Mary Seacole

A Story from the Crimean War

Sam Godwin

Illustrated by Alison Astill

an imprint of Hodder Children's Books

Mary Seacole (1805–1881)

1805 Mary Seacole was born 'Mary Grant' in Kingston, Jamaica.

1836 She married Edward Seacole.

1853 The Crimean War began.

1854 Mary travelled to England, hoping to go on to the Crimea in order to nurse British soldiers.

1856 The Crimean War ended and Mary returned to England.

1857 Mary wrote her best-selling autobiography, *Wonderful Adventures of Mrs Mary Seacole in Many Lands.*

1881 Mary Seacole died and was buried in London.

1990 The Jamaican government honoured the memory of Mary Seacole by giving her the Order of Merit.

Chapter 1
Lost and Hungry

I stood in the middle of a deserted street, trying to get my bearings. Where was I? Had I reached Balaclava? Or was I going round in circles, trapped somewhere near the city of Sebastopol, where the English and the Russians were slugging it out, tearing at each other with guns and cannons? I tried to clear my head but I was too hungry to think properly.

'Can I help you, son?' asked a passing soldier. 'You look lost.'

'I haven't eaten for ten days...' I began.

'I'm afraid I have nothing to give you,' the soldier said. 'But don't worry. You're nearly in Balaclava. Someone in the port will feed you.'

He doffed his cap and hurried on.

I waited a moment to gather my strength, then started walking again.

Balaclava was my destination. From there I could get a boat back home to Constantinople – once I'd scraped together enough money to pay my fare.

Suddenly I heard music. It was loud and
cheerful. People were laughing and clapping.
For a moment, I thought my mind was
playing tricks on me. How could anyone
be so cheerful in the middle of a war?

Then I turned a corner and saw warm
light spilling out of an open window across
the street.

SPRING HILL – THE BRITISH HOTEL

Next to it was a door with a British flag
fluttering on a pole above it. A sign said
'SPRING HILL – THE BRITISH HOTEL'.
Further along the wall were two more
windows. That's where the noise was
coming from. Someone was having a party.
I stopped in my tracks. Was that food I
could smell?

The aroma of cooking drew me across
the street like a magnet. I peeped through
one of the windows and saw a cook stirring
a pot. Behind him, cooling on a table,
were two freshly baked cakes. My mouth
watered at the sight of them. I just had to
have a piece.

Someone called out from another room and the cook left the kitchen, taking one of the cakes with him.

Slowly, I hauled myself over the window ledge. There was one cake left and I meant to lay my hands on it before it was taken away. Just as I was standing up, I heard a curtain being pulled aside and someone stepped into the room.

'What do you think you're doing?' demanded a loud voice.

Caught off guard, I swayed helplessly on my feet.

'Cake,' I said. Then I crashed to the floor.

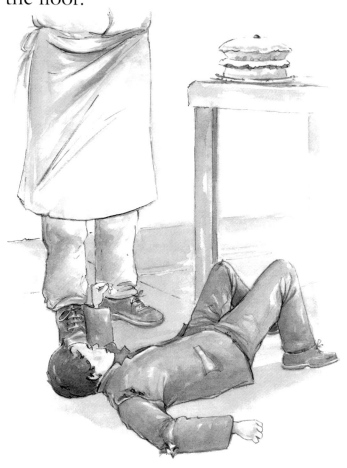

Chapter 2
A New Home and
a New Job

When I opened my eyes again, I saw two
people looking down at me. One of them
was the cook. The other was a big, fat
woman with brown skin and dimpled
cheeks.

'Hello,' she said. 'What's your name?'

'Omar,' I replied. While I'd been
unconscious, someone had lifted me on to
a warm bed in the corner of the kitchen.

'I'm Mary Seacole,' said the woman. She handed me some cake which I promptly started to wolf down.

'I think Omar likes our sponge cake, Moses,' Mrs Seacole said to the cook with a merry twinkle in her eye.

I'd never heard of sponge cake before, but it was the tastiest thing I'd ever eaten in my life.

'Now, Omar,' said Mrs Seacole. 'Is there anything else I can do to help you?'

'My father was killed near Sebastopol five weeks ago,' I said, 'delivering meat to the French troops on the front. So I'm on my way to Balaclava. From there I might be able to get a boat home. Only I don't have any money for the fare.'

'Why don't you work for me, then?' said Mrs Seacole. 'I'm very busy here. British soldiers come to eat at my canteen and to buy supplies from my shop. And when they are sick or wounded, I nurse them. Moses and I are worked off our feet. We could do with some help. I'll pay you a proper salary, of course.'

'We can't employ any street urchin who climbs in through the window,' protested Moses. 'We'll be robbed while we sleep.'

Mrs Seacole turned to me. 'Omar's not a thief,' she said firmly. 'He's just lost and hungry, that's all.'

'We're hungry too,' said a voice behind her. I looked up to see two young soldiers at the kitchen window.

'Any chance of a slice of cake, Mother?' asked one of them. He hiccupped and both men laughed.

'It's those two ruffians, Trimble and Jones,' sniffed Moses. 'They're drunk, as usual.'

'Why don't you go back to your
barracks, boys?' said Mrs Seacole gently.
'You'll be in trouble if a senior officer
sees you in this state.'

'We want some sponge cake,' repeated
Trimble. He looked at me and winked.
'You gave *him* some, Mother. It's not fair.'

Just then an officer called out from the dining room. Mrs Seacole said goodnight and left the room, followed by Moses.

Trimble belched and glared at me. 'So you're Mother Seacole's new pet, are you?' he said. 'Well, you watch out.'

I tried not to look scared. Soldiers. After what they'd done to my father I hated them all. I didn't care if they were Russian or British.

'Go away,' I growled, stuffing the last crumb of sponge cake into my mouth.

Chapter 3
Trouble with Trimble and Jones

'Why do the soldiers call Mrs Seacole "Mother"?' I asked Moses one morning. We were on our way to Balaclava to fetch supplies. I was now a trusted member of the household.

'Because she is like a mother to them,' replied the cook. 'No one cares more for British soldiers than Mrs Seacole. She came all the way to the Crimea from England to look after them.'

'Was she born in England?' I asked.

'Oh no,' said Moses. 'She was born in Kingston, Jamaica. But her father was Scottish. She learnt everything she knows about medicine from her mother. When she heard about the war, she wrote to the War Office to ask if she could come and tend the sick. But she was turned down. So she set up a business, came here with a relative and had the British Hotel built. In my opinion the hotel is too near the battlefield for safety, but Mrs Seacole insists she has to be close to her soldiers.'

I couldn't understand that. As far as I was concerned, all soldiers were murderers. I couldn't forgive them for killing my father and for bringing war to my country.

By now we had reached Balaclava. All around us, the streets were packed with people, mostly soldiers getting off their ships or tradesmen trying to sell goods. Moses left the cart outside an army depot and we made our way to the waterfront on foot.

'We're collecting a nice side of mutton,'
said Moses. 'Mrs Seacole is making a
special dinner for an officer tonight. It's his
birthday.' He elbowed his way through the
crowds until we reached a market that had
been set up on the quay. There we bought
the mutton, which the seller hung on a big
metal hook. Moses handed it to me.

'You take it back to the cart,' he said. 'I'm going to hunt around for some fresh eggs. Now make sure you look after it. Mrs Seacole has paid a small fortune for it.'

I nodded and started pushing my way through the crowds again. It was like swimming against the tide. People surged around me, elbowing and jostling, talking above the din and clatter of the market.

'Why, if it isn't Mrs Seacole's new pet!'

I turned to see Trimble and Jones grinning stupidly from ear to ear.

'Nice bit of meat you've got there,' said Trimble.

'For Mrs Seacole, is it?' asked Jones.

'It's none of your business,' I said.

'Don't be rude,' said Trimble. He lunged forward and snatched the meat from my hands.

'Give it back,' I yelled. Trimble ignored me and grinned at Jones. 'Come on. I know a couple of cooks who can make a lovely stew out of this.' And, before I could do anything else, the two rascals had disappeared into the crowd. For a moment I stood there, stunned. Then something inside me snapped.

'I hate you!' I screamed at everyone around me. 'I hate all of you!'

Chapter 4
Back to the British Hotel

I shivered. After losing sight of Trimble and Jones, it occurred to me that I couldn't go back to Mrs Seacole's. She might think I had stolen the mutton. Moses might even call the police. I didn't want to end up in a British prison.

So I wandered the streets of Balaclava, trying to think what to do next. After a while I collapsed in a doorway. The sun had set and I was sick with exhaustion.

'Why don't you go home, son?'

I looked up to see a British officer peering down at me from a hansom cab.

'I haven't got a home,' I retorted.

'You can't stay out here, it's going to snow,' said the officer. He nodded at the driver who got off his seat and helped me to my feet. I tried to fight him off but I was too weak. Besides, I was past caring. Even jail would be better than a frozen doorstep.

As the cab started to move again, I closed my eyes and leaned back in my seat. The leather felt warm against the back of my head. Now if only I could get something to eat...

'Omar, where have you been, my child? You had us sick with worry.' A familiar voice almost made me jump out of my skin. Mrs Seacole was looking in through the cab window.

I couldn't believe it. The officer had brought me straight back to the British Hotel.

'I didn't do it, Mother,' I blurted out.
'I didn't steal your mutton. Don't call
the police.'

'I never suspected you did, son,' said
Mrs Seacole. 'Now come out of the cold. I
have enough patients on my hands without
adding you to the list.'

I hobbled out of
the cab, stamping my
feet to get the blood
going again. 'It was
Trimble and Jones,'
I said, following her
indoors.

'Hush now,' she
said. 'You're back
home and that's
all that matters.
What's done
is done.'

That night, I lay on my bed in the kitchen trying to get to sleep. Mrs Seacole was making pies for breakfast, singing softly to herself as she kneaded the dough. I wondered how she could stay so cheerful when two soldiers had just robbed her blind. What was her secret?

Then I thought of Trimble and Jones feasting on the stolen mutton. Even if Mrs Seacole was ready to forgive them, I wasn't. Wait until I bump into them again, I thought. They'll regret ever crossing swords with me.

Chapter 5
A Terrible Day

A few days after the mutton incident,
Moses caught the flu. Over the next few
weeks, I was kept busy doing his chores as
well as mine. Every morning, Mrs Seacole
woke me up before dawn. Together, we
plucked the chickens, made coffee for the
soldiers and sold goods in the shop. After
lunch, we'd go to nurse the wounded in
the hospital across the road.

Sometimes Mrs Seacole would saddle her old donkey and ride to the battlefield with medicine and food. More than once I begged her to take me with her but she always refused. 'Children should not see the worst horrors of war,' she would say.

But one night, she did take me with her, and that night changed my life forever.

All that day, we'd been hearing cannon fire. The shelling never stopped for a moment. The road outside the British Hotel was full of carts bringing the wounded back from the front. The hospital across the road was full to overflowing. Mrs Seacole put aside her pots and pans and crossed the street to help the doctors.

When she came back, she was in tears.

'We have suffered terrible losses today,' she said. 'Come on, Omar. Let's go and see what we can do for the poor lads.'

I saddled two donkeys, and together Mrs Seacole and I started for the battlefield.

Chapter 6
Tending the Soldiers

I'd been close to the front before, helping
my late father deliver food, but nothing
had prepared me for what I was to witness
that night. As we approached the trenches,
I could see that the ground was covered in
men. Some were dead, others were calling
out pitifully, like small children, for their
mothers. It seemed there was blood
everywhere, running in dark streams.

Mrs Seacole got off her donkey at once. 'Child, the basket,' she said. I handed her the medicines and she set to work at once, sewing up wounds, bandaging broken limbs, holding medicine bottles to soldiers' lips. As we made our way through the sea of twisted bodies, voices would call out to her.

'Is that you, Mother?'

'God bless you, Mother.'

Mrs Seacole moved from one soldier to
another, working calmly, soothing their
pain with kind words.

All around us, cannonballs ploughed
into the soil. Bullets flew past our ears but
Mrs Seacole never flinched. I realized she
could not see the danger she was in. All she
could see around her were her children,
needing her help.

One of the wounded grabbed her by
the arm. 'Mother, help me,' he gasped.
I recognized that voice at once. It was
Trimble.

'I am here, my child,' said Mrs Seacole. She placed his head on her lap and, reaching in her basket, gave him some medicine to drink. Standing behind her, I could see that he was beyond help. A bullet had lodged itself in his chest and he had difficulty breathing.

'I'm sorry I stole your mutton, Mother,' whispered Trimble. 'I am a thief.'

'Hush now, you are not a thief,' said Mrs Seacole. 'You are lost and hungry, that's all.'

41

Those words cut through me like a knife. Wasn't that what Mrs Seacole had told me when I had tried to steal her sponge cake? I suddenly realized how foolish and arrogant I had been. Who was I to judge and condemn other people, inflicting my anger and hate on them?

In that instant, I also discovered the secret of Mrs Seacole's contentment. She did not see people's faults; instead she focused on their good points. That's what made her such a good nurse. And that was why so many strangers called her 'Mother'.

As I watched, Trimble held up his bloodied fingers to her face. 'You see, Mother,' he said, 'I cannot say goodbye to the ones at home, so I'll bid you goodbye for them. Perhaps you'll see them some day. If you do, just tell them I thought of them all – will you?'

'I will, my son,' whispered Mrs Seacole, trying her best to smile at Trimble. The soldier shivered once more and a moment later he was dead.

The poor man was only nineteen, not much older than me really. I stood up and took Mrs Seacole's hand. There was no hate left in me that night. It had seeped into the ground with Trimble's life – gone forever.

As the sun came up over the battlefield, I helped Mrs Seacole on to her donkey. 'Come on, child,' she said, wiping the tears from her eyes and starting to smile again. 'We have lots to do. There will be many new patients at the hospital today. And, if we have time, we'll bake something nice for the soldiers – to remind them of home.'

Glossary

barracks buildings where soldiers sleep

battlefield the place where a battle is fought

Crimea a piece of land on the Black Sea, taken over by Russia in 1783

depot a storehouse used for army supplies

officer a person of authority in the army

War Office a government department responsible for the British Army